THIS ~~UNG~~ LION • STORYBOOK

Holiday with the Fiend

Charlie Ellis lives next door to Angela Mitchell whom she once described in a class essay as "My Best Fiend". Angela is for ever having marvellous ideas but these often spell disaster, especially for Charlie who always seems to get involved. Living next door to Angela is one thing: having to share a holiday with her is quite another. Although Angela promises *not* to get Charlie into any trouble, things get off to a bad start when Angela dyes Charlie's hair . . . with disastrous results.

Charlie isn't the only person Angela plays tricks on – "drippy" Julian and the other odd assortment of guests at the Harbour View Hotel are on the receiving end of some of her most outrageous pranks ever. But, by the end of the holiday, Charlie is just a little bit fed up with Angela so, not above a little deviousness herself, she plots her revenge – with hilarious consequences.

Other titles available in Young Lions

SHEILA LAVELLE

Holiday with the Fiend

Young Lions

An Imprint of HarperCollinsPublishers

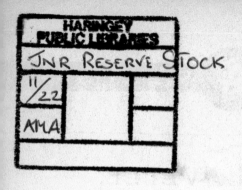
First published in Great Britain by
Hamish Hamilton Children's Books 1986
First published in Young Lions 1988
7 9 8

Young Lions is an imprint of
HarperCollins Children's Books,
a division of HarperCollins Publishers Ltd,
77–85 Fulham Palace Road,
Hammersmith, London W6 8JB

Printed and bound in Great Britain by
HarperCollins Manufacturing, Glasgow

Chapter One

THE letter for my mum came from the Hilton Hotel in London and was signed by somebody called Miss O. Bottom. My mum read it and then pushed it across the table towards my dad.

"Miss O. Bottom?" snorted my dad, peering at the letter through his glasses. "I bet her first name's Ophelia."

"Ophelia Bottom?" said my mum, not seeing the joke, and I laughed so much I sprayed

1

half-chewed bits of toast all over the table-cloth.

"That was a crummy thing to do," tutted my dad, and set me off all over again. My mum had to send me away from the table until I could get myself under control.

I didn't think it was fair that I should get into trouble while my dad just sat there grinning like a dolphin, but I got myself a drink of water and wiped my eyes and tried to calm down. When I came back to the table my mum was sitting there with a dreamy expression on her face.

"It would be heaven," she sighed. "Just to go off on my own for a change. Stay in a posh hotel. Look around the shops and have tea at the Ritz. No smelly socks to wash or dog hairs to clean up off the carpet. What bliss!" She jumped up suddenly and began to clear the table.

"I'd never go, of course," she said. "I couldn't leave you two on your own for a day, let alone a whole week." She started banging dishes about in the sink.

My dad began to read the letter out loud.

"'Cookery Summer School'," he said, putting on a posh voice. "'Stay at the world-famous Hilton

Hotel for a one-week course in French cuisine. Discover the secrets of our superb French chefs.'"

He licked his lips hungrily. "It sounds just the job. What do you think, Charlie, me bonny lass?" My name is Charlotte really, but everybody calls me Charlie, thank goodness.

"Mum doesn't need to go on a cookery course," I said. "She's the best cook in the world." To tell you the truth I thought it was a great idea.

"Creep," said my dad, out of the side of his mouth.

He had another look at the letter. "Look, Liz," he said to my mum. "There are still a few places left on the July course, starting next Saturday. If you really want to go, I can look after Charlie."

My dad poked me in the ribs. "How do you fancy a week's camping in the New Forest?" he grinned.

I was so delighted I shivered all over. There's nothing I like better than having my dad all to myself for a while. I could just imagine us roaming around in the woods with my dog Daniel, and I could already smell those sausages and beans sizzling over a wood fire.

"Ooh, Dad. It would be lovely," I spluttered, and sprayed more crumbs on the tablecloth.

"Don't talk with your mouth full, Charlie," snapped my mum. "How many more times do I have to tell you?"

Doesn't it make you sick the way they go on all the time? Don't talk with your mouth full and don't put your elbows on the table and don't gobble your food so fast and don't turn your fork upside down to shovel up your peas. What makes me really mad is that they do it themselves all the time. And if you dare to tell them so you're being cheeky.

My Uncle Barrie who lives in London says it doesn't matter how you eat your peas as long as you enjoy them. You can even have custard on them if you like, although I've never quite fancied that, somehow.

Anyway, my mum sat down again at the table and her face went all soppy and lighted up like it does when my dad brings her a bunch of flowers sometimes on a Friday night.

"I'd like to go," she said. "But you'd never manage without me."

"Of course we would," said my dad, giving her a kiss on the cheek. "It's high time you had a break. I think you should write back to this Miss Bottom woman before you change your mind."

And then I had to get up and go outside because my mum gave a sort of squeal and flung her arms round my dad's neck and started all that sloppy hugging and kissing stuff. It really gets on my nerves, I can tell you.

So I called Daniel from his basket and we went out to play in the garden. I'm trying to teach him to fetch a stick, but somehow I don't think he's very bright. He runs after the stick all right, and he even brings it back. But what he won't do is give it up for me to throw again. So I have to throw another stick, and Daniel picks that one up as well. After ten minutes or so he's got a hundred sticks in his mouth and there are none left for me to throw.

My friend Angela, who lives next door, says Daniel is the stupidest dog she's ever seen. She says he's stupid enough to run backwards and wag his head.

Anyway, I was sitting on the back doorstep trying to force Daniel's jaws apart to get the sticks out of his mouth when I heard footsteps hurrying up the drive and Auntie Sally appeared. She's not really my aunt, but I'm allowed to call her that because she's Angela's mum.

Auntie Sally looked pleased and excited, like a kid going to a party.

"Hi, Charlie," she said, smiling and ruffling my hair as she passed. "Your mum inside?"

"Yes, Auntie Sally," I said, hanging onto Daniel's collar so he wouldn't jump up and ruin another pair of her tights. "Just go in. She's in the middle of planning a trip to London. Some cookery course or other."

Auntie Sally grinned. "I know all about it," she said. "Your mum's just been on the phone. She thought I might like to go with her." And she pushed open the back door and went in.

I stared at the back door and frowned. I didn't think I liked that idea at all. If my mum and Auntie Sally went off to London together, then Angela might expect me and my dad to take her camping with us. And that would spoil everything.

It's not that I don't like Angela. It's just that she seems to have this awful habit of getting me into trouble all the time. She keeps playing horrible tricks on people, and it's always me that gets the blame. My dad says she's not a friend at all, she's a *fiend*.

Anyway, I left Daniel chewing up twigs on the doorstep and went inside to find out what was happening. And there they were, my mum and Auntie Sally, all thrilled to bits with themselves and yacking away non-stop about what they were going to do in London.

"What about Angela?" I interrupted, as soon as they paused for breath. "And Uncle Jim? What will they do while you're away?"

Auntie Sally smiled. "They can't wait to get rid of me," she said. "They're going off to the seaside for a week. Staying in a guest house near the beach with three good meals a day. They won't miss me for a second."

She turned back to my mum with a grin. "Right then, Liz? Let's get this letter written before all the places get booked up." And they sat down at the kitchen table with writing paper and envelopes and cups of coffee and started giggling away together like a couple of school-girls.

I was very relieved to hear about Angela's plans, I can tell you. But it didn't last long. Suddenly the back door was flung open and Angela marched in, her dad close behind her. They both looked dead pleased with themselves.

"Well, Ted," said Uncle Jim to my dad, who was busy drying the breakfast dishes. "These women of ours are gallivanting off on their own, are they?" He started waving a coloured holiday brochure under my dad's nose. "Just you wait until you hear what Angela and I have got lined up for you and Charlie." And he opened the brochure and began to read aloud about some place in Somerset called Shorelock Bay.

"Hang on, Jim," laughed my dad. "Charlie and I have made our plans. We're going camping."

"Camping? Rubbish. This'll be much more fun," said Uncle Jim. And as soon as he started talking about fishing, and golf, and tennis, and sailing, I could see that my dad was starting to weaken. Then, when Uncle Jim mentioned the pub just round the corner that sold the best cider in Somerset, I knew that all was lost. I sat on the window-seat and felt the sun warming my back through the glass, and I felt glummer and glummer the more I listened.

Angela came and sat beside me and put her arm round my shoulders. "Won't it be great?" she said. "You and me will have a fabulous time together, won't we?"

I looked at those great big blue eyes, all bright and sparkling with fun and mischief, and I had a horrible sinking feeling in my stomach like going down in a very fast lift.

"Let's go outside," I said grimly. "I've got something to tell you."

She meekly followed me out into the back garden and we parked ourselves down on the wooden bench under the apple tree. I took a huge deep breath and plucked up some courage from somewhere and I told her she was the last person in the world I wanted to go on holiday with. People went on holiday to enjoy themselves, I said, and if I had the choice I'd rather go with a killer whale.

Angela sat there with her mouth open and she

didn't say a single word until I'd finished. She stared at the ground for a long time and kicked at the daisies with the toe of her red sandal.

"What do you want, Charlie?" she said at last. "Have I got to promise never to play tricks on people again? Not ever?" Her voice sounded faint with disbelief.

"I only want you to stop getting me into trouble," I said. "It's always me that gets the blame. Why can't we have fun and adventures and stuff without causing trouble all the time?"

Angela said a rude word and tossed her long hair out of her eyes. "Adventures?" she scoffed. "Who, you? Your idea of an adventure is to eat After Eight Mints at half-past seven." She got up and scowled down at me, her hands on her hips. "You know who you remind me of, Charlie Ellis?" she said. "The Incredible SULK." And she danced away and started doing handstands on the lawn.

I could see that I wasn't getting anywhere, but I had no more time to argue because just then the grown-ups all came out to tell us that the whole thing had been decided. And of course it was just what I had been dreading. My dad and Daniel and I weren't going camping after all. We were going to Shorelock Bay with Angela.

They all stood around on the patio, talking and laughing and saying what a great plan it was and not one single person thought of asking me what I thought about it. Not even my dad. And that's what hurt most of all.

"What about Daniel?" I shouted suddenly, blinking away the tears. "They won't allow dogs in boarding houses, I bet. And I'm not putting him in kennels, so there."

"No problem, Charlie," said Uncle Jim cheerfully, waving the brochure under my nose. "It says small, well-behaved dogs are welcome at no extra charge. We'll take his basket along and he can sleep in your room." And they promptly forgot all about me and started arguing about whose car they were going to take.

Angela took one look at my sullen face and then marched over to stand in the middle of them all.

"Charlie doesn't want to go," she announced in a loud voice.

They all stopped talking and turned round to

stare at me and I could feel my face going as red as tomato soup.

"Why ever not?" said Auntie Sally, looking astonished.

"I . . . er . . . well . . . I didn't exactly say that," I stammered, feeling dead embarrassed.

"She doesn't want to go with *me*," said Angela. "She says she'd rather go with a man-eating shark."

"I didn't say shark. I said whale," I told them crossly. "I said I'd rather go with a killer whale."

And, would you believe it, they all fell about laughing as though it was the funniest thing they'd ever heard.

"I can't say I blame you," said my dad, wiping his eyes. "Angela, you'd better make a solemn vow to be on your best behaviour. Then maybe Charlie will change her mind."

There was a silence as Angela stared gloomily down at her feet. Then she looked up and smiled one of her radiant smiles. The sort that makes all her dimples show.

"All right, I'll try," she said bravely. And everybody clapped and cheered as if she'd won a gold medal or something.

Well, after that I couldn't go on sulking, could I? I had to give in and just make the best of it and keep my fingers crossed that it would all turn out right in the end.

I really should have known better, though, because she started her tricks before we even set off.

Chapter Two

IT was Friday, the last day of term and the final bell had just gone. We were all messing about in the school corridors, collecting coats and satchels and shoebags and stuff, and saying goodbye to all the friends we wouldn't be seeing until September. I looked round for Angela so we could walk home together, but she was surrounded by a crowd of boys, as usual.

"Hang on a second, Charlie," she called. "I'm

just getting a few addresses. Come and hold some of my things for me, will you?"

I pushed my way into the middle to see what she was up to. And there she was, her face all pink and pleased, scribbling down the names and addresses of all the boys who were begging her to send them postcards. And even though I'm not usually jealous of her being the most popular girl in the class, I couldn't help feeling a bit of a twinge because nobody had asked me to send them a card. Not even that nice David Watkins, who wants to marry me when I grow up. He was busy writing down his address for Angela, too.

I slung Angela's shoebag over my shoulder and picked up a few more of her belongings, including a big ball of string she'd brought to school for an art and craft lesson.

"Shall I send you a card as well, David?" I said hopefully, giving my best smile and batting my eyelashes the way Angela does. All I got was a sort of half-hearted nod.

"If you like," he said, as if he couldn't really care less. "Angela's got my address."

Angela giggled and I felt my face go red. I

hunched my shoulders and trudged off towards the school gate. But it wasn't long before she came hurrying after me.

"What's up, Charlie?" she said, pulling me round to face her. "You won't be seeing David for a while, is that it?" She tucked her arm through mine and gave it a squeeze. "Never mind, there's plenty more fishes on the beach. I bet there'll be hundreds of nice boys at Shorelock."

"I bet they won't like me, though," I said gloomily. "They'll like you best. They always do. It's not fair." In a sudden fit of temper I shoved her things into her arms. "You can carry your own shoebag from now on," I said. "*And* your stupid ball of string." And I stalked away in a huff.

"Don't be like that, Charlie," called Angela, running to catch me up again. "It's not my fault, is it? How can I help it if boys like me best?"

"You're prettier than me," I scowled, as if it was a crime. "And anyway, you've got blonde hair and I haven't."

Angela stared at me very hard and her eyes started to go that funny green colour like they do when she's having one of her ideas.

"We can easily do something about that," she said gleefully, and she began to drag me along the street towards the town centre.

"There. What about that, then?" Angela said suddenly, stopping in front of the chemist's shop and pointing dramatically at a display in the window.

I stared at the display. There was a mountain of coloured boxes of something called Blondex. For only seventy-five pence it promised to change your whole life.

"'Don't envy those beautiful blondes,'" read Angela from the advertisement in the window. "'Be one yourself. Just comb Blondex cream into your hair, leave for thirty minutes and rinse out. You will be delighted with your shining golden locks.'" She gave me a hard nudge in the ribs. "How about it, Charlie? Dare you?"

I kept on staring at the window and my chest felt all sort of funny inside. There was a picture of a gorgeous girl like a film star with long golden hair all around her shoulders, leaning against a red sports car. And there was this fabulous bloke in a bow tie and a posh dinner jacket gazing at her the way my dad gazes at a pint of beer. That could be David Watkins, gazing at me, I thought dreamily.

"Of course I dare," I said, taking a deep breath. "But I haven't got any money. I've put it all in the bank for my holidays."

"That's no problem," said Angela jubilantly, and she marched me into the shop.

One of the nice things about Angela is that she's never mean with her money. She gets loads more pocket money than I do, but she's as generous as anything with it. She's always buying me ice-creams and Mars bars and stuff like that. And she handed over seventy-five pence for that Blondex cream without batting an eyelid.

We came out of the shop and my stomach felt a bit funny.

"My mum and dad will go mad," I said, and my voice came out all sort of weak and faint. "Especially my dad. He likes my hair the way it is."

"We won't tell them, stupid," said Angela. "We'll do it tonight, just before you go to bed. They won't see it until tomorrow morning. And by then it'll be too late." She gave a snort of laughter and danced about on the pavement. "Don't forget our mums have to be on the train at seven-thirty. They won't even have time to look at you."

We were carrying so much stuff that at first we couldn't find anywhere to put the Blondex, but in the end I managed to squeeze the box into my shoebag and we set off home. We had just reached the corner of the High Street as a posh bloke with white hair and a tweed overcoat was coming out of the Post Office.

"Hang on, Charlie. Watch this," giggled Angela suddenly, a gleam in her eye. "We'll have some fun with this old codger and this ball of string. I'm sick of carrying it anyway."

I stood on the pavement holding her satchel and her shoebag and watching in astonishment as she went trotting up to the old gentleman.

"Excuse me," she said, smiling politely. "I wonder if you could help us for a minute? My friend and I have to measure the length of the High Street with this ball of string. If you just wouldn't mind holding one end for a few minutes . . .?" And she smiled up at him and flapped those long eyelashes.

"School project, is it?" said the man. "Glad to help. Only hope you've got enough string." And he cheerfully got hold of the loose end.

"Come on, Charlie," said Angela, grinning at me and she started walking backwards along the High Street, unwinding the string and smiling encouragingly at the old man as she went.

"What are you up to?" I hissed at her. "You know we haven't been given any such project. You'll get us into trouble."

"Shut up, Charlie, for cripes' sake," she said. "Can't you see it's only a joke?" And on she went, paying out more and more of the string, until the old gentleman was only a dot in the distance.

The string ran out just as we turned the corner near the fish shop. A fat woman with baggy red trousers and a face to match was just coming out. Angela gave her one of her most charming smiles.

"Excuse me, madam," she said. "We are doing a school project. We need someone to just hold the end of this string for a moment. Would you mind?"

The fat woman put down her shopping bag.

"Not at all," she said, beaming. "Don't mind a bit. I just have to hold it? Is that right?"

"That's fine," said Angela, and I could tell she was trying not to giggle. "Just keep it tight, if you can. We'll be back in a minute. Thanks very much."

We went haring off down the next street, and as soon as we were a safe distance away Angela started to fall about laughing. And of course I couldn't help joining in.

"I wonder how long they'll stand there?" gasped Angela, wiping her eyes on her hanky. And we collapsed in a helpless fit of giggles.

Well, we got home eventually and parted at my front gate, Angela promising to come round later that evening. I crept upstairs and hid the box of Blondex at the back of my wardrobe, and I suddenly got this awful feeling in my stomach. As if I was on my way to the dentist for ten fillings. I sank down on my bed and I sat there and thought about it for a long time and in the end I decided that turning blonde was a stupid idea after all. I would tell Angela I'd changed my mind the minute she came round. And as soon as I'd decided that I felt a whole lot better.

When I went downstairs I found my mum in the kitchen. I got a bit of a shock when I saw her because her eyes were all red and runny and she kept dabbing them with her shirt sleeve and sniffing. Something awful must have happened, I thought. Maybe the cookery course had been cancelled. I couldn't help hoping it had.

"Don't cry, Mum," I said, putting my arms round her waist. But she only laughed and pushed me away.

"I'm not crying, silly," she sniffed. "I'm just chopping these onions. I'm cooking our favourite supper, as it's our last evening together for a while. And I've still got loads to do."

I'd never seen the house look such a shambles. There were half-packed suitcases lying about the place and piles of ironing still to finish. I peeled some potatoes to go with the steak and onion pie, then I finished packing my own suitcase and started helping Daniel with his.

"Charlie," said my mum in disgust. "You're not taking all that rubbish, surely?"

"Dad said I could," I said quickly. "I want Daniel to settle down and feel at home, with his own things around him."

My mum just shrugged her shoulders and got on with the ironing, leaving Daniel and me in peace. It's amazing how often you can get your own way, when one parent tells you not to do something, by saying that the other one said you could. You'd think they'd have the sense to check more often.

Anyway, Daniel and I got on with packing his old brown blanket and his rubber bone and his ball and his spare collar and lead and his condition tablets and his plastic dinner dish and his water bowl and his box of biscuits and seven tins of Meaty Chunks. And last of all we put in his old chewed teddy bear with no arms and no legs and no eyes and no ears that Daniel loves better than anything else in the whole wide world.

It all took rather a long time because Daniel decided it was more fun to take things out of the bag than to put them in. But we got everything packed eventually, just as my dad came home from work.

He was grinning and whistling and he was in such a daft mood that my mum asked him suspiciously if he'd been to the pub.

"Now would I do a thing like that?" he said,

his eyes going wide and innocent. "I've brought home a nice bottle of plonk so we can all have a drink together."

He opened the wine at suppertime and we all drank a toast to a happy holiday while we ate our steak pie and potatoes and peas. My dad often lets me have half a glass of wine with a meal, but my mum always makes me put water in it which ruins the taste. I bet she wouldn't like it if she had to put water in hers.

After supper my dad did the washing-up while I helped with the drying.

"Thanks, Charlie," Mum said, smiling at me. "We seem to be getting organised at last. I've just got a few odds and ends left to iron, while you pop upstairs and have your bath. Don't forget to wash your hair as well."

"Aw, Mum. Do I have to?" I said, making a face. "Angela's coming round. We're going to play Scrabble in my room."

"That's all right," said my mum. "You can play Scrabble in your dressing-gown and pyjamas."

So I finished drying the last few plates and things and went upstairs for my bath. I made jolly sure the bathroom door was shut properly, because last time I left it slightly open and Daniel got in. He took one look at the water and then leaped straight in on top of me. We got rather a lot of water on the floor, and my mum wasn't very pleased about that, I can tell you.

I was just wrapping a towel round my clean wet hair when I heard Angela's voice downstairs.

"Come straight up, Angela," I called, leaning over the banister. "I've been washing my hair."

"Oh, good," said Angela, opening the door to my bedroom. "We can get straight on with it then."

I sat down on the bed and began to rub my hair with the towel.

"Where've you put the stuff?" said Angela. "I can start getting it ready."

I peered out at her through a small gap in the towel.

"I'm not going to do it," I said faintly. I had a feeling she'd blow her top.

"You're what?" she squeaked incredulously, and my heart sank.

"I'm not going to do it," I mumbled again.

"I've changed my mind." And I started rubbing my head hard so I wouldn't have to look at her.

There was such a long silence that in the end I had to look. And the funny thing is, she wasn't furious at all. Only disappointed.

"I might have known you'd chicken out," she said wearily. "But I don't think it's very nice of you, Charlie. Not after I spent nearly all my money on getting that stuff for you. Sometimes I wonder why I bother with you at all." And she started towards the door.

I couldn't help feeling that maybe she was right and I suddenly felt ashamed. She must think I'm a right drag, sometimes. I decided to show that once in a while I could be wild and adventurous, too.

"Wait," I said, taking a deep breath. "Come on, then. Let's get it over with."

Angela grinned and started capering about the way she always does when she gets her own way.

"You won't regret it, Charlie," she said. "You're going to look fantastic."

So we got out the carton of Blondex and I sat on my dressing-table stool while Angela combed that horrible thick smelly cream through my hair.

"You haven't half got a lot of hair, Charlie," she complained after a while. "It's taking a lot of stuff. We should have bought two lots."

I stared at my reflection in the mirror. Half my hair was sticking out in greyish greasy spikes, while the other half was as dark and curly as ever.

"What are we going to do now?" I wailed. "It's too·late to get any more."

Angela grinned at me in the mirror. "Don't panic, Charlie," she said. "I'm sure my mum's got some stuff at home. She once put some blonde streaks in her fringe. Just hang on, and I'll see if I can pinch what's left."

She left me sitting there and hurried off. I wrapped my head in the towel in case anybody came into my room. I was beginning to wish Blondex cream had never been invented.

Before long Angela was back, waving a bottle with some pale yellowish liquid.

"What's that?" I said suspiciously.

"Well, it's not Blondex," she said. "But it's the same sort of thing. Peroxide or something. I'm sure it's just as good."

Anything was better than leaving my hair as it was, so I let her take the towel off and dab the yellow stuff all over the other half of my head.

"There," said Angela, looking at her watch when it was finished. "It's ten past seven now. So we have to rinse it off at twenty to eight. Let's have a game of Scrabble."

We got rid of the mess and hid the empty bottles and cartons in the bottom of my wardrobe. I wrapped the towel round my head and got out the Scrabble board.

"Rude-word Scrabble or ordinary?" said Angela, shaking up the plastic letters in a bag.

"Ordinary," I said quickly. Angela always wins at rude-word Scrabble. I suppose I just don't know enough rude words.

It didn't take us long to get interested in the game, and I started winning straight away because Angela's such a rotten speller. I was just making her take back NUCKLE when it suddenly dawned on me that the half-hour must have been up ages ago.

"Angela, the time," I squealed. "We forgot about the time."

Angela gave a little shriek the way her mother

does when Daniel puts his muddy paws on her skirt.

"It's after eight o'clock," she said. "Quick, get in the bathroom and rinse that stuff off."

I put my head in the washbasin and Angela started to pour jugfuls of hot water over my head.

"Ouch," I said. "That's blooming hot."

"Stop moaning, Charlie," said Angela impatiently. "I wish I never said I'd help."

Anyway, we managed to get all the stuff rinsed off eventually and I rubbed my hair dry on a clean towel. Then I sat down in front of my dressing-table mirror to admire the result.

"Oh," I said weakly. "Oh, lord."

Angela didn't say anything. She was too busy rolling about on the bed, stuffing her hanky in her mouth and clutching her stomach and shrieking.

"It's not FUNNY," I shouted, staring at myself in the mirror. "It's the most horrible mess I've ever SEEN."

It was, too. The side of my head that been Blondexed was a ghastly shade of yellowish green, while the other side was a yucky brassy orange. And right through the middle was a broad stripe of dark brown hair that Angela must have missed altogether. I looked a proper freak.

"Go away, Angela," I said, tears coming into my eyes. "Just go away and leave me alone. I don't care if I never see you again."

Angela slid off the bed and tried to wipe the grin off her face.

"Sorry, Charlie," she said. "I couldn't help it. You don't half look funny." And I could hear her giggling all the way down the stairs.

I put the Scrabble away and crawled miserably into bed. And when my mum came to say good-night I put my head under the covers and pretended to be asleep. I didn't know what on earth I was going to do in the morning.

But Angela must have been really sorry for me after all, because later that night when everybody was asleep I heard some gravel being thrown against my bedroom window.

I got up quickly and leaned out and there was Angela in her slippers and pyjamas, grinning up at me in the moonlight.

"Here, Charlie. Catch this," she said. "I know you'll look super in it."

She threw into my open window her best cream straw hat with the brown velvet ribbon on it that she wore at her baby cousin's christening. And it must have been a real sacrifice because I know she loves that hat better than anything else she owns.

She really can be as nice as pie sometimes. It's just a pity that it doesn't happen a bit more often.

Chapter Three

"DO you have to wear that stupid hat at the breakfast table, Charlie?" said my mum irritably, and I clutched it tightly to my head in alarm.

It was the next morning and we'd all been out of bed since the crack of dawn. My mum was rushing about like a mad thing, throwing last minute odds and ends into her case and trying to do her hair and put on her make-up and swallow her toast and coffee all at the same time.

"It's not a stupid hat," I said defensively. "It's Angela's very best sun hat. She gave it to me for my holidays."

"Oh, let her wear it, Liz," said my dad, picking up the breakfast plates and taking them to the sink. "She's not doing any harm. You just concentrate on catching that train on time. You can safely leave Charlie to me for a while."

"Yes, well, I hope you both manage to behave yourselves," said my mum. But she didn't make me take the hat off and I gave my dad a grateful look.

Anyway, a minute later she had forgotten all about it, because Auntie Sally suddenly appeared at the back door. And Uncle Jim, who was taking the two mums to the station, was tooting his horn in the drive.

"'Bye, love," said my mum quickly, giving me a brief hug and a kiss on the cheek. "Have a lovely holiday. Keep an eye on your dad." She grabbed her case and her handbag, ruffled Daniel's ears, and then she was gone.

I felt a bit funny, I can tell you. I'd never had to do without my mum for a whole week before and I wasn't sure if I could manage without her.

But then my dad came in after seeing them off. I looked at his kind face and his brown eyes that blink all the time like a short-sighted teddy bear and I knew that everything was going to be all right.

It was going to be a long drive to Shorelock, so I took Daniel for a good run in the park near the river while my dad finished the washing-up. When I came back Angela was there, helping her dad and mine to load all the gear into the car. Angela had on a pair of pink trousers and a pale pink satin sun top with bare shoulders. She stared at my tatty old T-shirt and jeans.

"Are you going like that?" she said, screwing up her face.

"Why not?" I said. "We've both got to sit in the back seat with Daniel for five hours. What's the point in wearing good clothes?"

Daniel was dancing round the car enjoying all the excitement and Angela gazed in distaste at his muddy paws.

"That spaniel had better keep his filthy feet off my new trousers," she said crossly. "They cost nearly twenty quid at Harrods'." She grinned at me suddenly.

"You look great in that hat, Charlie," she said. And of course I couldn't help grinning back.

Uncle Jim's car was filled to bursting with all our luggage. There were suitcases, canvas bags, golf clubs, beach balls, fishing rods, tennis rackets, Daniel's basket, rugs and picnic hampers for fine days and jigsaws and Scrabble for wet ones. Plus a few million other things as well.

"That's the lot, girls," said Uncle Jim. "See if you can squeeze into the back. I'll just check the oil and water." He stuck his head under the bonnet of the car, while my dad went off to lock up the house.

Angela and I started to get into the back seat with Daniel when a shout from the gate made us both turn round.

"Good grief," said Angela, trying not to look pleased. "It's that stupid fat fool, Laurence Parker. And that nice David Watkins. What on earth are they doing here?"

"We've come to see you off," called David, shuffling his feet and looking dead embarrassed.

"Have a nice time, Angela," said Laurence Parker, pushing David out of the way. "Don't forget to send us a postcard."

"We won't forget," Angela called back. And then she did a really rotten thing. It was so unexpected I didn't have time to stop her. She reached across and yanked the straw hat off my head and left me standing there with my green and orange and brown stripey hair all uncovered.

I gave a shriek and tried to grab the hat back. But I was too late, anyway. The boys had already noticed my hair.

It didn't have quite the result Angela was hoping for, though. The two boys came closer, staring away like anything, and you should have seen the expression on their faces. Just like the man in the Blondex advertisement.

"Wow," said David Watkins admiringly. "Charlie, your hair's fantastic."

"You look real punk, Charlie," said that stupid fat fool Laurence Parker. "It's really ace."

I glanced at my reflection in the car window and I saw that it didn't look too bad, after all. A bit like something off *Top of the Pops*, I suppose.

"Oh, thanks. Do you really like it?" I smiled, shaking my hair about and showing off.

Angela stepped over to me and shoved the

straw hat so firmly back on my head she almost broke my neck.

"Get in the car, Charlie," she snapped furiously. "We can't stand around here all day."

I climbed into the back seat with Daniel and I had a good old giggle at the expression on Angela's face. Our two dads got in as well and Angela slid in beside me and stared straight in front of her. And she didn't even wave as we all set off down the drive and turned into the street. I wound the window down on my side and hung out of the car, waving like mad, until the boys were out of sight.

"That Laurence Parker's a fat, sweaty nit," said Angela suddenly. "And David Watkins is a right creep."

I didn't say a word. I just smiled quietly to myself and stroked Daniel's silky ears.

Uncle Jim drove steadily through the country lanes, and it wasn't long before we reached the motorway to the West. My dad kept telling silly jokes and singing funny songs and pretty soon Angela was starting to cheer up. She never seems to sulk for long, and anyway nobody could stay grumpy on a lovely sunny morning with the sky all blue and the larks singing and the thought of a week's holiday by the sea. I was careful to keep Daniel at the other side of me so he wouldn't accidentally muddy Angela's clothes, and after a little while she began to thaw out and giggle a bit at my dad's daft antics.

She had got over her sulks completely by the time we stopped for an early lunch at the motorway service station, and she even tucked her arm through mine as we walked from the car. We knew Daniel wouldn't be allowed in the restaurant, so we let him have a little run on the grass and then shut him back in the car with a drink and a handful of biscuits. I made sure the car window was open enough to let in some fresh air.

"Off you go and wash your hands, girls," said my dad. "We kind fathers will get us a place in the food queue."

There were a lot of people about as it was the first day of the school holidays and everybody seemed to be going somewhere. We even had to queue for the ladies' loo, and that's what must have given Angela her awful idea. When we came out she was walking ever so slowly and thoughtfully, and her eyes had that strange, sparkly look that they get when she's planning something.

"Come on, Angela," I said, trying to hurry her along. "My stomach's rumbling like mad."

"Hang on a minute, Charlie," she said. "I just want to get something from the shop." And she disappeared into that sort of newsagent place that sells sweets and magazines and postcards and stuff.

I groaned to myself and followed her inside. If she was up to something I supposed I'd better find out what it was.

I found her buying an enormous great sheet of white card and a thick black felt-tip pen. I looked at them in astonishment and Angela giggled.

"What on earth do you want those for?" I said. "You'll never get them in the car. Not that great lump of card, anyway."

"It's not going in the car, stupid," said Angela. "You go on ahead and find our dads. I'll catch you up in a minute. OK?"

"No, it's not OK," I said crossly. "You're going to play one of your tricks, aren't you,

Angela Mitchell? And I want to know what it is."

Angela grinned a very nasty sort of grin and put her face right up close to mine.

"You don't really want to know, Charlie," she said. "You don't want to get into trouble, remember? So off you go like a good little girl and find your daddy. Because wicked Angela Mitchell is going to do something very naughty indeed." And she cackled like a witch on Hallowe'en night.

I felt like giving her a good hard kick on the shin and I could feel my face going red. But I turned round and marched away with my head in the air. Let her get herself into trouble if that's what she wants, I said to myself. I didn't want anything to do with it.

I found my dad and Uncle Jim about halfway up the long queue in the cafeteria.

"Hullo, where's Angela?" was the first thing they said.

"Oh, she's coming," I mumbled, waving my hand vaguely towards the door. And would you believe it, she appeared less than a minute later,

smiling all over her face. There was no sign of
the sheet of card and I felt relieved. Maybe she
hadn't done anything after all.

"Changed your mind?" I hissed into her ear as
she joined us in the queue. But she only shook
her head and tossed her hair and refused to tell
me anything.

"I'm absolutely starving," was all she said.
And you should have seen her loading her tray.
Chicken pie, chips, roll and butter, orange juice
and a great big slab of chocolate gâteau with
cream. I decided to enjoy my lunch, too, and not
to worry about her any more.

"So'm I," I said cheerfully, piling another tray
with the same sort of stuff.

"Be careful, girls," warned my dad. "We don't
want anybody being sick in the car, do we?
You're often a bit car-sick, Angela, I seem to
remember."

"That was last year," said Angela scornfully,
"when I was just a kid." And she added a slice of
apple pie to her loaded tray.

Well, she chatted and smiled all through lunch
and she kept on bursting into peals of laughter
for no reason at all as far as I could see. I kept

staring at her in alarm, wondering if she was laughing at me still wearing my straw hat. But it was only when we had finished lunch and were outside again that I found out the real reason.

In the car park next to the ladies' loo there was the most enormous crowd of women, all shouting and arguing and milling about in confusion.

"Good lord," said my dad. "What's going on here? It's like the January sales."

We walked past the entrance to the loo on our way back to the car, and Angela suddenly gave me a hard nudge in the ribs.

"How about that, then, Charlie?" she whispered gleefully. "I managed to put it there when nobody was looking."

I stared, and my mouth fell open in astonishment. For there was Angela's great sheet of card, leaning against the door of the ladies'.

And scrawled on it in big black letters was this notice:

THESE LAVITORYS ARE
TEMPERAIRILY OUT OF ORDER.

Chapter Four

MRS DOWN stared at Daniel as if he was something slimy from under a stone.

"That dog is not allowed in any of the public rooms," she said, in a posh voice that sounded as if she was trying to talk like the Queen. "And of course especially not in the *dayning*-room."

We were standing in the hall at Harbour View with all our belongings piled up in a heap on the doorstep outside. There was a horrible stink of polish and disinfectant, and I could see that

Daniel wasn't going to be popular if he came in with muddy feet or shed hairs on the carpet. Even the sniffy young housemaid who'd let us in looked red and scrubbed as if she'd washed herself with the lavatory brush.

Mrs Down, the landlady, was just as clean and shiny as her house. She was plump and pink and smelled of soap and talcum powder, and I wondered if she had a bath three times a day.

My dad gave Mrs Down one of his most charming smiles.

"Don't worry, my dear Mrs Down," he said soothingly. "We'll see that Daniel behaves himself. I expect we'll be out most of the time anyway."

"That's all right then," cooed Mrs Down, falling for my dad's charm like all women do. "And make sure the little girls play in the back garden, won't you, Mr Ellis? Not in the front. The front garden is my own special little retreat, and I like to keep it *prayvate*."

She patted her blue-rinsed perm into place. "Now, let me show you your rooms," she said. And, watching the floor anxiously in case we were bringing in any dirt, she led the way upstairs.

It was one of those big old houses with lots of staircases and landings and funny dark corridors leading off in different directions, and it took ages before we finally stopped at a bedroom on the second floor.

"Rooms twenty-one and twenty-*fave*," said Mrs Down, handing my dad two keys with wooden labels tied to them. "Twenty-*fave* is along the landing and around the corner." She smiled round at us all politely. "The evening meal is at six. Do please *tray* not to be late." And she bustled away, flicking imaginary dust off the banister as she went.

Of course we'd already had the argument about who was going to share a room with who. Angela had wanted me to share with her and let the two dads have the other twin-bedded room. But I wasn't having any of that, I can tell you. Being stuck with Angela all day was going to be bad enough. I didn't want to be stuck with her all night as well. And for once I actually got my own way. My dad and Daniel and I were to have room twenty-one, while Angela and her dad had number twenty-five along the corridor.

"We'll go off and explore the beach in a little

while," said my dad, unlocking the door to our room and pushing it open. "But let's get all our luggage upstairs and unpacked first, eh, Charlie? Then we can relax and enjoy ourselves." And with the two of us working it didn't take long, my dad carrying the stuff upstairs and me unpacking it and putting it away in cupboards and drawers.

The room was very clean but nothing special. There were two rock-hard narrow beds with pale green crocheted covers, two chests of drawers, and a great big wardrobe that was all dark and spooky inside as if a skeleton lived in it.

A card was stuck on the wall telling you the rules of the house, like not using too much bath water and not making a noise after nine o'clock and not making muddy footprints on carpets and not letting dogs jump on beds.

"It's just like being at home," I said to my dad, and he burst out laughing. "Do you think Mrs Down's first name might be Ida?" I asked him, and he laughed even harder.

"Nice one, Charlie," he said. "And I bet her two sons are called Ben and Neil."

When we'd finished all the unpacking I put

Daniel on his lead and went along the landing to see how Angela and her dad were getting on. I found Uncle Jim unpacking all by himself.

"Angela went off to explore the garden," sighed Uncle Jim ruefully. "Never mind, I can do it quicker myself, anyway." And he went on putting stuff away in drawers.

I went down all those twisty stairs and out into the back garden. And there was Angela, wearing her new white sundress and sandals, swinging idly on a swing and talking to a pale spotty boy in specs who looked about our age.

"Hey, Charlie," she called, when she saw me. "Come and meet Julian. He's been here a week already. And guess what, he's crazy about his computer. He even brought his with him."

I wondered what the boy was staring at as I walked over the grass towards them with Daniel. But I soon found out.

"I like your sun hat," he said, and I put my hand up to the brim in surprise. I'd forgotten I had it on, to tell you the truth. I suppose it did look a bit strange with my old T-shirt and jeans. Especially as the sun wasn't even shining.

"This is Charlie," Angela told the boy with a

giggle. "You know, the one I was telling you about. And that is her daft spaniel called Daniel. Charlie's got this horrible disease that's made all her hair fall out. She's got to wear her hat all the time because she's as bald as a banana."

The boy stared even harder and I felt myself go hot all over.

"That's a stinking rotten lie and you know it," I shouted. "You can keep your stinking rotten old hat." And I snatched the hat off my head and flung it at her . . . just as my dad and Uncle Jim came out into the garden to look for us.

Angela's blue eyes danced with glee. My heart turned over three times and sank like a stone into my plimsolls.

"Now you're for it," hissed Angela, and I could see she couldn't wait to watch me getting into trouble.

My dad just sort of gaped at me in horror at first and started to say something that might have been a very rude word. The one my mum has made him promise not to say any more. But then I think he realised from my red face how upset I was, because he suddenly managed a weak grin.

"Well, bonny lass," he said, coming over and

putting his arm round my shoulders. "You look a right bobby dazzler, I must say." He led me a little way away from the others. "Madame Angela's work, I suspect?" he said quietly. "I thought so. Never mind, kid. We'll get it fixed before you go home. OK?"

And that was all he said. I nodded and gave him a squeeze round the waist and I felt so grateful I could have cried. So to relieve my feelings I put my tongue out at Angela instead. And all she could do was glare at me because it seemed that everybody liked my weird hairdo, after all. Even Uncle Jim was whistling in admiration.

Anyway, the sun had come out again so off we went to explore the little town of Shorelock, with its fishing boats tied up in the tiny harbour and its narrow pebbly beach. Daniel raced up and down the shore barking madly at the waves and telling the seagulls that this was his beach now and they'd better stay off it, or else.

Drippy Julian came with us and bored us to death talking about computers. He couldn't understand that we hadn't got one and didn't even want one and we had an awful time getting him to talk about anything else. But at last Angela managed to make him tell us about Harbour View and some of the other guests and that was much more interesting.

The first thing he told us was that the house was supposed to be haunted, which made Angela clutch at me in fright with her eyes round as dustbin lids. Then he said that one of the guests was a Russian spy.

Angela kept gurgling and saying oh and ah, but I was beginning to think this Julian person was making it all up just to impress us. I didn't believe a word of any of it, and I'm sure Angela was only pretending to.

As we strolled up into the High Street we passed one of those stupid joke-shops that sell stink bombs and exploding cushions and rubber snakes and stuff like that. I hate that sort of thing, but of course Angela gave a squeal of delight and immediately disappeared inside. I couldn't follow her in because a sign on the door said dogs weren't allowed, so all I could do was stand outside and wonder fearfully what it was she was buying. I hoped it wasn't a giant plastic spider like the one she'd put in my bed when I was staying at her house once. I woke everybody in the whole street with my screaming, and Auntie Sally wasn't very pleased, I can tell you.

I didn't get a chance to ask her about it when she came out of the shop because that drippy Julian suddenly grabbed our arms and hissed at us excitedly.

"That's him over there," he whispered. "Mr Borovski. The Russian spy."

A small man with wild black hair and a beard was hurrying down the steps of the Maritime Museum. He was muttering away to himself in a very peculiar way, and he kept stopping to scribble things down in a small black notebook. He jumped like a frightened grasshopper when Julian called good afternoon to him, and scuttled off round the corner as if he thought we were going to mug him or something. He really was the most suspicious-looking person I had ever seen.

"He really does look like a spy," I said.

"He is, I tell you," said Julian. "I've been following him. He goes in the museum every day and copies battleship plans and navigation charts. I'm sure he's working for the Russians."

Angela gave that tinkly little laugh of hers. The one she's copied from somebody on the telly. I've heard her practising it when she didn't know I was listening. She thinks it's ever so attractive, but I think it's just silly, if you ask me.

"He could even be one of them aliens," she said. "From outer space. Maybe they're planning an invasion."

"He's a spy, stupid. I know he is," said Julian, and they immediately started an argument. But they didn't have time to argue long, because we suddenly realised that our two dads had disappeared into the distance and we had to run to catch them up.

We found them at the bus station looking up the timetable of buses to Shorelock from Lynton, another little seaside town about ten miles along the coast. They were making plans for a long hike on the following day, and you should have heard Angela's moans and groans.

"Ten miles?" she said, screwing her face up in horror. "You must be joking."

"We're quite serious," said Uncle Jim, waving his map about and getting all enthusiastic.

"Look, we'll walk from here right along the cliff path. The views will be absolutely fantastic. We can take a few sandwiches for lunch and then come back on the bus in the evening."

"But I can't possibly walk ten miles," wailed Angela. "Aw, Dad. Do Charlie and me have to come? We'd much rather just play on the beach. Wouldn't we, Charlie?"

"Rubbish," laughed Uncle Jim. "It'll do you the world of good. Some good brisk exercise is what we all need. Right, Charlie?"

I thought it was a great idea. I like long country walks, especially by the sea. And I knew Daniel would love every minute of it. But poor old Angela sulked all the way back to Harbour View.

We met the other guests in the dining-room at teatime, and they had no call to stare at me and my hair because they were a right funny-looking lot themselves.

Sharing our long table near the bay window was Mr Borovski, not speaking to anybody and looking shiftier than ever, turning his salad over suspiciously with his fork as if he thought it might be full of caterpillars. There was a young

Dutch student called Peter, on holiday to improve his English, who stood up and bowed every time a lady came into the room. He seemed to be on some sort of diet of hard-boiled eggs, and he had a most peculiar little habit. The eggs would be waiting on his plate when he came into the room, and he would crack them by banging them against his forehead. When Angela saw this she laughed so much she nearly fell off her chair, and her blue eyes started to sparkle like they do when she's having one of her ideas.

There were two schoolteacher ladies, one tall and thin and grey-haired with wrinkled brown skin like corrugated paper, and the other short and sort of square with pale watery eyes and freckled hands and big white teeth like tombstones. They both wore proper leather walking boots and thick socks and they parked their rucksacks in the corner before they sat down.

Also sharing our table were that drippy Julian and his parents, Mr and Mrs Fisher, who were both pale and weedy and wore glasses like their son. Mr Fisher had straight black hair that stuck up like the bristles on a shaving brush, but Mrs Fisher wasn't so bad. In fact, she would have been quite good-looking if it hadn't been for her moustache. All the Fishers gobbled their food as if they hadn't eaten for a week, and Angela said they probably hadn't.

The food was great and there was plenty of it, ham and salad and pickles and new potatoes and fresh crusty bread and butter. On the sideboard along one wall I could see what looked like bowls of peach trifle, so I made sure I left some room. And it was while we were waiting for the pudding to be served that the awful thing happened. The most horriblest, awfullest, most embarrassing moment in my whole life. Even worse than that time when my grandad got a coughing fit in that posh restaurant in London, and my dad banged him on the back so hard that his false teeth shot out into his chicken soup.

Mrs Down and the maid were clearing away the first course and the maid was sniffing away as usual. I wondered if she had a bad cold or hayfever or something, or whether she just sniffed from habit. Maybe she was trained to sniff out dust and dirt, the way police dogs sniff out bombs and drugs and stuff.

Anyway, I was thinking about this and not

taking any notice of the conversation round the table when suddenly I felt Angela gripping my arm in a panicky way.

"Charlie," she whispered urgently. "Has Daniel been in here?" And she had the most horrified expression on her face that I had ever seen.

"What?" I said, staring at her. "Daniel? Of course not. He's upstairs in his basket. Why?"

Angela glanced quickly round to make sure nobody was listening. Then she rolled her eyes downwards and pointed a finger towards the floor.

"Well, he must have got in somehow," she breathed. "Look what's under the table."

I couldn't think what she was on about, but I leaned slightly back in my chair until I could see the floor. What I saw there made the blood rush to my face and my knees turn to strawberry jelly.

"Oh, lord," I groaned. "Daniel hasn't done that since he was a puppy. It can't have been him."

"There's no other dogs here," Angela pointed out. "Who else could it have been?"

I knew she was right, but I still couldn't

understand how Daniel had got in, or when. He must have sneaked downstairs when I was in the bathroom or something, I supposed.

I peered down again at the thing on the floor and I could feel my face going from red to white and back to red again. Right in the middle of Mrs Down's nice yellow carpet it was, too. She'd have a fit if she saw it. I would have to do something before that happened. The question was, what?

My dad was sitting opposite and I started to try to catch his eye. But he was much too busy chatting up the younger of the two school-teachers, the fat one, and telling her the best kind of polish to use on her hiking boots. He didn't even notice me wiggling my eyebrows at him frantically over the table, and when I tried to kick him on the shin I got Julian instead.

"Ouch," said Julian, glowering at me. "What was that for?"

"Er . . . nothing," I stammered, and Angela sniggered. "It was an accident, honest."

I went cold all over when Mrs Down came in carrying a pile of pudding plates. Any minute now, I kept thinking to myself. But Mrs Down was too busy serving the peach trifle to notice what was on the floor. She plonked a huge bowlful in front of me and I couldn't even say thank you. My voice didn't seem to want to work.

Angela scoffed all her trifle and licked her spoon. She looked greedily at my untouched plateful.

"Poor Charlie," she said, and I could tell she thought the whole thing was dead funny. "Don't you want your trifle? I'll eat it if you like?"

I let her take it. Right then I didn't care tuppence about peach trifle. I kept staring anxiously at the floor, waiting for everybody to finish their meal and go away so that I could clean it up, and praying that Mrs Down wouldn't notice anything before I got the chance.

Angela finished my trifle and scraped the plate noisily.

"Luvverly," she sighed, smacking her lips. "Pity you've lost your appetite, Charlie."

And then she did the most amazing, astonishing thing. I was so surprised that all I could do was sit there like a village idiot with my mouth hanging open. Sometimes she's the best friend in the whole world, I told myself.

Angela took her lacy little hanky out of the pocket of her new white sundress, and at the same time she dropped her pudding spoon on the floor.

"Oops. Silly me," she said, and quickly dived under the table. Then, while pretending to be only picking up her spoon, she rapidly scooped that nasty little mess into her hanky and slipped it into the pocket of her dress.

"There," she said with a grin, scrambling back into her chair. "Panic over. All right now, Charlie?"

I didn't know what to say. I felt so relieved that tears came into my eyes. I tried to give her arm a grateful squeeze but she just pushed me off.

"It's OK, Charlie," she smiled. "I just don't want you getting into trouble, right?"

I went with her into the garden when that dreadful meal was finally over and I've never been so glad to get out of a room in my life. I thought the first thing Angela would do would be to empty that thing out of her pocket and dump it on the compost heap. But to my astonishment she unwrapped it from her hanky and started bouncing it about on the concrete path. She giggled helplessly when she saw my face.

"You really are a dope, Charlie Ellis," she said. "You really believed it was real, didn't you?"

It was only then that I remembered the joke-shop she'd called into that very afternoon. How could I have been so stupid?

I stood there for a minute as she danced around me crowing with laughter. Then without stopping to think I grabbed her by the hair and dragged her across the lawn and shoved her in the smelly old goldfish pond, new white sundress and all.

It didn't half make a mess of her dress. She was so furious she didn't speak to me for the rest of the day. But it was worth it. She really does drive you mad, sometimes.

Chapter Five

IT never takes Angela long to get over her sulks, and she was as nice as strawberry jam next morning when I met her on the landing before breakfast, as I was bringing Daniel back from his early morning walk.

"Come on, Charlie," she said with a grin. "Let's bury the hatchet."

If I'd had a hatchet I know where I'd like to have buried it, I can tell you. But she looked so excited and pleased with herself that I couldn't help wanting to know why.

"What's up with you?" I said, shooing Daniel into the bedroom and into his basket. "You look like the cat that pinched the kippers."

"I've been up ages, making plans," Angela replied, hopping about from one foot to the other. "Just wait until you see the fun we're going to have in the dining room at breakfast time."

I gave a loud groan. "Oh, Angela," I sighed. "Not again. Why can't you just behave yourself for once?"

"Pooh to that," she said, flicking her long hair out of her eyes. "I'd be bored out of my mind. And so would you." She looked at my worried face and tucked her arm through mine.

"It's only a couple of little jokes," she said, in the wheedling voice she always uses to get her own way. "It's not against you this time, honest. And it's nothing that'll get you into trouble, I promise."

"Cross your heart and hope to die?" I said, scowling suspiciously.

Angela crossed her heart and fervently hoped

to die, so I let myself be hurried away downstairs to the dining room.

There was nobody about as the breakfast gong hadn't yet been sounded. Angela sat down at the table and started to write something on a piece of paper that she took from her pocket. I looked over her shoulder to read it.

"WE KNOW WHAT YOU'RE UP TO!" it said.

"What's that for?" I asked, baffled, and she chuckled.

"For Mr Borovski," she said. "To find out if he's really a spy or not." And she folded the note and slipped it under the cup and saucer at Mr Borovski's place.

The breakfast gong sounded in the hall, and I heard people starting to come downstairs and in from the garden. I went to my seat, but Angela took something else from her pocket and fiddled with one of the plates at the end of the table.

"Hey, that's Peter's place," I said. "You're not playing tricks on that nice student, I hope."

She slipped into her chair just as our two dads and the other guests began drifting in.

"It's nothing terrible, Charlie," she giggled. "You'll see."

I didn't have to wait long. As soon as everybody was sitting down and Miss Sniff had started to bring round plates of sausages, bacon and tomatoes, Peter the student picked up one of the hard-boiled eggs that were waiting in his place as usual. Angela nudged my arm.

"Watch this," she whispered, wriggling with excitement.

Peter bashed the egg smartly against the front of his forehead, to crack it in his usual funny way. But instead of just cracking, the shell smashed into bits and runny egg started to slide down the astonished student's face in a horrid slimy mess.

"Mine heavens!" spluttered the student. "It is an raw egg. It has not even cooked been." And the yellow yolk dripped slowly off his nose onto the tablecloth.

Angela stuffed her table napkin into her mouth and choked with laughter. I could feel myself going bright pink from trying not to laugh, too, especially when the skinny one of the two schoolteachers tried to mop Peter up and only made it worse. In the end the student had to go away and wash his face properly, while everybody hid their grins and said what a shame it was and how on earth could it have happened.

They all decided it must have been a mix-up in the kitchen and poor Miss Sniff got the blame. The only person who thought it might have been a joke was Peter himself.

"I think somebody has been trying to take off my leg," he said when he came back to the table, and Angela choked all over again. The student cracked all his eggs very carefully with a knife after that, you can be sure.

During the rest of the meal Angela and I kept an eagle eye on the other end of the tables as well, but Mr Borovski still hadn't noticed the note under his saucer. It was only when Mrs Down came round offering more tea or coffee and he moved his cup slightly towards the teapot that he saw it.

I gave Angela a nudge and we watched as our suspected spy drew the note quickly into his lap. He opened it under the edge of the table and stared down at it and his face went as pale as a pudding under his beard. He licked his lips nervously and stared round at everybody's face to see who was looking at him. Angela and I were very busy at that moment putting sugar in our tea and stirring it.

Suddenly there was a loud clatter as Mr Borovski pushed his chair back and ran from the room.

"Funny man," said Angela. "I wonder what can be the matter with him." And her blue eyes danced with glee.

Our two dads were still dead keen on this plan of theirs to hike along the coast, so as soon as Angela and I had finished breakfast they sent us off to get ready.

"Jim and I will just have one more cup of coffee and finish off the toast," said my dad, settling back in his chair. "You two can go and chat up Mrs Down and persuade her to pack us a picnic lunch."

Angela groaned. "I think we should call the whole thing off," she said, going to the window and peering out. "Look at that black sky over there. It's going to pour."

"Rubbish," said Uncle Ted, glancing towards the window. "I can see lots of blue sky. It's obviously brightening up. Off you go and get those sandwiches organised, eh?"

I was really looking forward to a day's hiking, but Angela grumbled all the way down the passage to Mrs Down's kitchen.

"Who wants to go on a rotten old hike?" she said, scowling. "They must be mad. This is supposed to be a holiday, not a survival course."

The landlady wasn't in the kitchen and Miss Sniff didn't know where she was, so we decided to go and look for her outside. We couldn't find her in the back garden, nor the front, but we found something else that made Angela stop and stare, her face going suddenly thoughtful.

"I've got an idea, Charlie," she said slowly. "If this works, we needn't go on that stupid walk after all."

All I could see was a garden sprinkler, spraying water on Mrs Down's flowerbed. I couldn't see how that was going to help. But Angela was slipping through the small gate into the landlady's special private garden, with its plastic gnomes and rabbits and windmills and red and white spotted toadstools.

"Quick, Charlie," she urged me. "Run and

turn the hose off at the tap near the side door. I'm going to move the sprinkler."

I raced round the corner and did as I was told, and when I came back I found Angela dragging the sprinkler across the lawn and turning it so that it pointed towards the front of the house.

"OK, turn it on again," she grinned, and as soon as I did so I realised what she was trying to do, because suddenly a great deluge of water shot out of the sprinkler and started cascading against the dining-room window.

"That should do it," giggled Angela, quickly shutting the front gate with its large PRIVATE notice. "Now let's see what they've got to say."

The other guests had all gone and the tables had been cleared. My dad and Uncle Jim had the footpath map spread out in front of them but were sitting gazing ruefully at the window and the water drumming heavily against the glass.

"We couldn't find Mrs Down," said Angela. "Oh, goodness. Is it raining? Do you still want to go?"

My dad shook his head. "No point in getting drenched," he sighed, disappointed. "We'll leave it for a while. See if it clears up later on."

"Right, then," said Angela, grinning at me triumphantly. "Me and Charlie will play Scrabble upstairs." And then she did a very clever thing. "Shall we bring you the chess board down?" she suggested slyly. She knows as well as I do that they'd be there for hours if they got started on a game of chess.

My dad looked at Uncle Jim, who nodded and looked more cheerful at once.

"Good idea," said Uncle Jim. "It's time I gave you a thrashing, isn't it, Ted?"

Angela whooped with glee as she raced up the stairs. I followed more slowly, feeling a bit fed-up. I didn't fancy being stuck in the house all day. But Angela had other plans.

"We can spend the whole morning on the beach," she said. "I'll buy you the biggest ice-cream we can find."

"Can I bring Daniel," I pleaded. "I promise I won't let him jump up on you." And she was so pleased with herself that she said yes.

I put Daniel on his lead while Angela ran downstairs with the chess set. Then we set off together down the road towards the sea.

It had rained a bit in the night and now it was a

coolish sort of day with a chilly breeze. The air smelt lovely and clean and fresh, and I took great big gulps of it as we went along. It made my head spin as if it was Champagne. Angela was wearing red shorts and red sandals, a beautiful new cream velvet jacket with big pockets, and a red silk scarf tied round her neck, cowboy-style. I had jeans on and my battered old green anorak and I could tell she thought I looked scruffy by the way she kept glancing sideways at me as if I had a blob of custard on the end of my nose. But I didn't care. I was happy and comfortable, and glad just to be out in the fresh air.

We played on the beach for a while. I threw stones into the sea for Daniel to chase while Angela amused herself by writing some not very polite words in the damp sand with a stick. The two frumpy schoolteachers from Harbour View came along and they couldn't believe their eyes. They tutted like anything and hurried away, muttering about how awful children were these days and whatever was the world coming to.

Angela pretty soon got bored with that stupid game, however, and started pestering me to go with her for ice-cream. She didn't like me throwing pebbles for Daniel because every time he came out of the water he shook himself and sprayed water everywhere.

"Make him stop, Charlie," she squealed, shrieking and leaping out of the way. "This jacket cost twenty-four pounds."

She got her own way as usual, and off we went for another walk along the sea front. It wasn't long before the sea breeze started to make me feel hungry and it seemed a heck of a long time since breakfast, so I didn't object when Angela pulled me into one of those open-air beach cafés to buy me the ice-cream she had promised. She looked around for a place to sit and grinned happily when she spotted two empty chairs. And who should be sitting at the same table but those same two schoolteachers from the boarding-house.

"Couldn't be better," giggled Angela, pushing me down into one of the seats. "You wait there with Daniel while I get the ice-creams." And she came back a few minutes later, smiling all over her face, and carrying two of the most enormous ice-creams you ever saw in your life.

They were in tall narrow glasses about a foot

high and there was everything in them you could think of. Cherries, nuts, grated chocolate, chopped fruit, fresh cream and three kinds of ice-cream, chocolate, strawberry and vanilla.

"Flippin' heck!" I breathed. "That doesn't half look good."

"You'll never eat all that," warned the thin schoolteacher primly. "You'll spoil your lunch." Angela gave her a withering look and started tucking in.

We had those posh long-handled spoons to eat them with, and they were the most delicious ice-creams I've ever had in my whole life. Daniel lay on the sandy floor under my chair looking mournful because he's not allowed to beg at the table, but I did manage to slip him a bit of chocolate when nobody was looking.

The two ladies sipped weak tea and watched disapprovingly as I scoffed my way rapidly down to the bottom of the glass. At last I put down my spoon with a sigh and wiped my sticky mouth on my hanky.

"Thanks, Angela," I said. "That was great."

I was surprised to see that she'd only managed to eat about half of hers. She was gazing at it moodily, and stirring it around into a horrible sloppy mess with her spoon.

"You were right," she sighed, smiling at the two ladies with that innocent look of hers. "I can't manage it, after all. I think I'll have to save the rest for later."

She put down her spoon and stood up. Then, to everyone's astonishment, she carefully opened the pocket of her brand-new expensive cream velvet jacket, and very slowly poured all that sloppy melted ice-cream straight into it.

I wasn't the only one to be horrified, I can tell you. People at the other tables were nudging one another and gaping, and I could see one of the waiters staring with his mouth open in amazement.

The two schoolteacher ladies were gawping at Angela as if she was something from outer space. I shrugged my shoulders helplessly as Angela burst out laughing and made for the door.

I grabbed Daniel's lead and we raced after her. There she was out in the street, leaning weakly against a lamp-post and shaking with giggles.

She grabbed me when she saw me and danced me round and round on the pavement.

"Oh, Charlie," she gasped. "Wasn't it the funniest thing you ever saw? The look on their faces."

"It wasn't that funny," I said grumpily. "And you've spoiled that good jacket, too. You can't really think it was worth it." I looked for the messy stain I expected to see seeping out of her pocket, but the jacket looked as clean and neat as ever.

"I'm not that stupid," said Angela scornfully. "I had the whole thing planned. Look, Charlie. I had my pocket lined with this." She opened her pocket and pulled out a big plastic bag.

"Here you are, Daniel," she said, kneeling down on the pavement where he was sitting with his I-haven't-been-fed-for-a-fortnight face. "I've saved you some lovely ice-cream." And she opened the bag so that Daniel could lick it clean.

I could hardly stay grumpy with her after that. So we linked arms and started to saunter back to Harbour View for lunch, making up silly poems and jumping over all the cracks in the pavement as we went.

The sprinkler was still spraying the dining-room

window when we got back, and Angela looked pleased.

"I bet they're still playing chess," she said with satisfaction. "If you just pop round the side and turn the water off, Charlie, I'll move the sprinkler back to where it was before."

She slipped through the gate into the front garden while I went round the corner and turned off the tap.

"OK," I called, and stood by the tap to wait for her to shout for me to turn it on again.

And that's when I suddenly had an idea of my own. I don't know what came over me, because I don't usually play silly tricks on people. But it was just too good an opportunity to miss.

I peeped round the corner to make sure she had picked up the sprinkler and was carrying it back to the flowerbed. Then I ran back and turned the tap on as hard as it would go.

I stood in the drive and capered with glee as the sprinkler suddenly leaped like a wild thing in Angela's hands and then drenched her from head to foot in cold water.

"Ow! Charlie!" she shrieked. "Turn the bloomin' thing off, for Pete's sake.

I did so, but by then she was soaked to the skin. Her cream velvet jacket was dripping wet, and her hair hung limply round her face like wet washing.

"Coo, sorry, Angela," I said meekly. "I thought you said turn it on." But of course I wasn't a bit sorry really. It was great to get my own back for a change.

She gave me such a filthy look I thought she was going to kick me. But she only pushed past me and flounced off into the house and up the stairs. And when she came down again in dry clothes she forgave me at once, because our two dads were still engrossed in their game and her plan had been a complete success.

"Hallo, had a nice morning?" they asked absently. "It seems to be brightening up at last." And Angela winked at me and grinned.

I thought somebody would remark on her soaking wet hair when they all came trooping in for lunch but nobody even noticed. They were all too busy discussing the strange disappearance of Mr Borovski, who'd packed his bags straight after breakfast and rushed off with still almost a week of his holiday left.

Chapter Six

THE sun was streaming in the bedroom when we woke up next morning. I hopped out of bed and opened the curtains and saw that the sky was a brilliant blue.

"Angela's got no excuse this morning," puffed my dad, doing press-ups in his red and white striped pyjamas. "It's a perfect day for a walk."

Angela had realised there was no getting out of it this time, and she seemed quite cheerful when she came along to my room in her red shorts, her white sun-top with the narrow shoulder-straps, and new white plimsolls and ankle socks. I was wearing shorts too, and my best Save Our Hedgehogs T-shirt, but my dad made me wear my oldest, most comfortable canvas trainers.

"It's a long hike, pet," he warned. "You want something comfortable on your feet."

Angela and I went downstairs together for breakfast, and she couldn't wait to tell me all about her latest plan.

"You know this place is supposed to be haunted?" she said, her eyes gleaming like they always do when there's trouble ahead. "Well, I've had a great idea."

"I don't believe it's really haunted," I said. "It's only that drippy Julian trying to be funny."

"That's just the point," giggled Angela. "We'll teach him a lesson. We'll get dressed up as ghosts and creep along to his room in the middle of the night and frighten the socks off him."

I didn't like the sound of it at all. "He'll scream the place down," I said. "We won't half get into trouble if we're caught."

Angela sighed. "You're not much fun any

more, Charlie," was all she said. But I knew she hadn't given up the idea, because she pestered Julian with questions about the ghost all the time we were eating breakfast.

"It's a white lady in a long gown," Julian told her, speaking quietly so nobody else would hear. "It's supposed to walk the corridors at night, moaning and sighing and wringing its hands."

"Who told you about it?" I demanded suspiciously, and that drippy Julian looked dead pink and uncomfortable.

"Oh, I just heard it somewhere." he said vaguely. And I was positive he was making it up.

My dad had chatted up Mrs Down and persuaded her to make us each a picnic lunch.

"What about coming with us, Julian?" invited my dad, picking up the four parcels of food from the sideboard. "The fresh air will be good for you."

Julian had so far spent the whole of his holiday in his room playing with his computer. His skin looked white and doughy, like something that lives under a stone.

"No thanks, Mr Ellis," he said politely. "I'm in the middle of writing a very interesting program, and I'd like to do some work on it if you don't mind."

His mum and dad smirked at him adoringly. You could tell they thought their son was a genius. Maybe he was, but he was also a right bore, and I was glad he wasn't coming with us.

My dad and I had already packed our rucksacks with waterproof jackets and spare socks and a sweater in case it turned cold. I had put in my little watercolour paintbox and a sketchpad as well in case we found a nice view. All we had to do now was put in the food and we were ready to go.

I ran upstairs and fetched Daniel, and when I got back down into the hall I found Angela and her dad having an argument because she didn't want to carry her own things.

"I haven't got a proper rucksack," she said sulkily. "I can't possibly carry everything in this stupid little bag."

"All right," sighed her dad. "Put your stuff in my rucksack and I'll carry it for you."

And at last we all set off down the High Street towards the sea, with Uncle Jim bent almost double and Angela skipping along, all smiles because she'd got her own way.

But she didn't smile for long. We were passing the window of the Shorelock Saddlery and Hardware Store when my dad stopped and pointed to some nice little canvas rucksacks in the window.

"That's just the job for Angela," he said. "Come on, kid. I'll buy you one."

Angela glared at him, but she couldn't very well refuse. So my dad and I slipped off our rucksacks and, leaving them on the pavement with Uncle Jim, we went into the shop.

"Yes, help yourself," said the assistant, when we asked about the rucksacks in the window. My dad started sorting through the pile to find one the right size, and that must have been why the posh lady with the blue hair thought he was the shopkeeper.

"Excuse me, my good man," she asked him haughtily, "do you keep doormats?"

My dad looked at her for a moment and a twinkle came into his eyes.

"Yes, madam," he grinned. "I've got six at home in a cage."

Then he snorted with laughter as the lady's face

went as red as a tomato and she rushed out of the shop. It's a good job my mum wasn't there or he'd have got a right telling-off, I can tell you. He really is as bad as Angela sometimes.

Anyway, we got Angela's stuff transferred into the new rucksack and settled it comfortably on her shoulders. Then we set off once more.

And for the first mile or two it was great. The path took us up the cliffs with the sea on our right, and as we climbed higher the view became more and more spectacular. All sorts of birds were singing in the bushes around us and there were more wild flowers than I had ever seen before. We marched along enjoying the sea breeze and laughing at Daniel's antics as he scampered about chasing imaginary rabbits.

But I might have known it wouldn't last long. Pretty soon Angela started to lag behind. She was too hot. We were all going too fast for her. Her new shoes were hurting her feet. The rucksack straps were rubbing her bare shoulders. She was hungry. She was dying of thirst. And so on, and so on, and so on.

After a while Uncle Jim grew tired of her moaning and threw down his rucksack.

"OK. You win," he said. And even though it was only eleven o'clock, Angela insisted on eating her lunch.

"It'll make the rucksack lighter to carry," she explained reasonably. And the fresh air had made us all so hungry that we could do nothing but agree.

After ham sandwiches and sausage rolls and lemonade our two dads lay flat on their backs in the sun while I sat a little way off and got out my paintbox. There was a red sailing boat with white sails in the bay below us, and it made a lovely picture with the sparkling blue sea.

Angela sat beside me to watch.

"You are clever, Charlie," she said admiringly. "I wish I could paint like that."

"It's not all that good, really," I said modestly, even though I thought it was the best painting I'd ever done. "Here, have a go. It's easy." I tore a page off the pad for her and lent her a brush.

She painted happily for a few minutes. Then she swore and screwed the paper into a ball.

"I'll never be an artist," she sighed moodily, tossing the paper over the cliff. "My dad says I can't even draw the curtains."

"Litter lout," I sniffed reprovingly and she giggled.

"Sometimes you sound just like your mum," she said.

Angela watched idly as I mixed some lovely washes of purple and green and blue for the sea.

"That's giving me an idea," she said thoughtfully. She glanced quickly over her shoulder at our dads, who were still resting in the sun with their eyes closed. Then she pulled off her right shoe and sock.

"What on earth are you doing?" I said in alarm, as she took a brushful of purple, green and blue paint and started daubing it all over her ankle.

"You'll see in a minute," she said, blending in a touch of yellow and putting her head on one side to admire the effect. "There. That should do it."

She waved her foot about until the paint was dry. Then she carefully put her sock and shoe back on.

I was mystified, but it wasn't long before I found out what she was up to. We'd all set off again and had walked about another half mile.

Angela was walking in front with Daniel when she suddenly seemed to lose her footing. She gave a shriek and tumbled sideways off the path down a little slope.

"Ow, my ankle," she yelped. She sat up and clutched at her foot and screwed up her face in pain.

My dad and Uncle Jim didn't bat an eyelid. They were getting used to her complaints by now.

"Come on, you'll live. It's only another seven miles," said my dad cheerfully. And if looks could kill he would have dropped dead on the spot.

We went a bit further, and Angela bravely struggled on, limping on her bad foot and sometimes on her good one as well. We had to keep stopping to wait for her and eventually Uncle Jim sighed.

"What a kid," he said. "I suppose it's just possible she's really sprained her ankle?"

"Better have a look," advised my dad. "Just to be on the safe side."

Angela sat down on the grass and painfully eased back her sock. Both our dads gasped at the horrible purple bruise she showed them on her ankle.

"Good lord," said Uncle Jim. "You must be in agony. You poor kid." And Angela nodded, bravely blinking back the tears.

My dad tried to feel her foot to see if anything was broken, but she whimpered so much that in the end he had to leave it alone.

"It seems to be only a bruise," he said. "But she'd better not try to walk on it any more. We'll have to carry her back."

And so that was the end of our lovely long walk. My dad and Uncle Jim linked hands and staggered back along the clifftop all the way to Shorelock with Angela perched precariously between them. It took a long time because the path was narrow and they had to pick their way, and they were hot and red and sweaty when we finally reached the town. I could have killed her for ruining our nice day out, and I was feeling pretty worn out myself. I had to carry Angela's rotten rucksack.

"I could murder a pint," muttered my dad, as we passed the pub near the beach. "But I suppose we'd better get Angela to hospital for an X-ray."

Angela wriggled to the ground.

"It's not broken, Uncle Ted," she said earnestly. "In fact, it feels a lot better now. Charlie and me can sit on the beach while you go for a cider."

"Well, if you're sure . . ." said Uncle Jim uncertainly, looking longingly at the doorway of the pub.

Angela tested her foot on the ground and tried hobbling a few paces.

"Look, it's better," she said. "It only needed a rest. Come on, Charlie. Let's go and lie in the sun." And she began to limp across the road towards the beach.

When our dads came back to look for us half an hour or so later I was paddling in the sea with Daniel, and Angela was sunning herself lazily in a deck-chair. She had taken her shoes and socks off, and I saw my dad suddenly pick up one of her socks and look at it suspiciously.

"Come on, Angela," he said. "We'll go for a paddle. The cold water will be good for your bruise."

"That's a good idea," said Uncle Jim, pulling Angela to her feet. "Uncle Ted's right. Cold water's the best thing in the world."

Angela screamed and struggled, but between them they half-dragged, half-carried her down to the edge of the water. And of course it only took a few seconds for the waves to wash every trace of watercolour from her foot.

Uncle Jim stared at Angela's ankle in astonishment, but my dad just nodded wisely as if he'd suspected something funny all along.

At first she tried to brazen it out.

"Gosh, Uncle Ted, you were right," she said, gazing at her foot as if she'd never seen it before. "Look, the bruise has completely gone."

"Fancy that," said my dad. "It's nowt but a miracle. Marvellous what a drop of seawater can do."

"All right, Angela," said Uncle Jim, folding his arms grimly. "I want to know exactly what's been going on."

And so Angela had to confess the whole thing. She hung her head and said how sorry she was and shuffled her feet and went red in the face. And instead of being furious as I'd expected, they both roared with laughter.

"Whatever will that child get up to next?" said Uncle Jim, shaking his head admiringly. We all set off up the road to Harbour View for tea, with Angela skipping and dancing as if nothing had happened, and me trudging along behind, scowling my head off.

It makes you wonder how she manages to get away with it sometimes. I reckon Shorelock cider must be pretty good stuff.

Chapter Seven

THE trouble with Angela is that she very easily gets bored. She's not content to read a book or paint a picture or knit herself a scarf. She has to be plotting and scheming and causing trouble all the time, and the more people she can find to play her tricks on, the better she likes it.

A holiday boarding-house is a great place for somebody like Angela, and she didn't waste a single chance. She put big black plastic spiders in all the bathrooms, and frightened the two lady schoolteachers out of their wits. She pinched all the room keys off the board in the hall and muddled the numbers up before hanging them back on the wrong hooks. And one night she even crept into the larder while everybody was asleep and changed all the labels round on the boxes and tins of food. So there was salt in the sugar container and flour in the rice jar and peaches in the tins labelled baked beans. It made some of the meals a bit of a surprise, I can tell you.

I kept on refusing to have anything to do with her plans, and finally she stopped pestering me to help her and just got on with it herself. I was relieved not to be getting into trouble, but at the same time I couldn't help feeling a bit glum that I was missing all the excitement. It doesn't seem fair that the wicked people in the world have all the fun.

One morning Daniel and I came back from our early walk and caught her sneaking out of the dining-room with one of her dad's muddy hiking boots on the end of a long pole. I stared at her in astonishment, and Daniel growled at the boot fiercely as if it was about to attack it.

"Shurrup, you stupid dog," hissed Angela. "You'll wake everybody up." And she shoved the boot into a carrier bag and hurried away upstairs.

I peered round the door into the dining-room but I couldn't see what she had been up to. I didn't find out until we were all sitting at breakfast and Angela kept giggling so much she could hardly eat her scrambled eggs on toast.

"Look at the ceiling," she whispered, when I begged her to tell me what was going on. I glanced upwards, and I almost choked.

Right across the white-painted ceiling from the doorway to the window were great big black muddy footprints. I looked fearfully at Mrs Down, but she was serenely serving coffee and fluttering her eyelashes at my dad.

"The rules say no muddy boots on the carpets," murmured Angela slyly. "They say nothing about the ceiling, do they?" She gave her tinkly little laugh. "I bet you anything you like that nobody notices," she said. "People just don't look at ceilings."

And do you know, she was right. I sat there fiddling nervously with my breakfast expecting that any minute somebody would give a shout. But not one person even glanced upwards, not during that breakfast or at any other meal for the rest of our holiday. As far as I know those muddy footprints are there to this day.

After breakfast our two dads went off for a game of tennis. Angela and Daniel and I sat on a rug in the garden to write postcards. One of Angela's tricks when she's on holiday is to send people cards from invented characters they've never even heard of. Our PT teacher, Miss March, keeps getting seaside scenes with messages like, "Having a lovely time. Wish you were here. Love, Daisy and Tom."

Angela gets a good giggle out of all those poor people puzzling their brains out for weeks on end wondering who on earth Daisy and Tom are, but I think it's a waste of postcards myself. I sent mine to all my friends at school, including that nice Nicola Daley and her pretty little sister, Leanne. And of course I sent one to that dishy David Watkins who's going to marry me when I grow up if Angela doesn't grab him first.

I had kept the nicest card of all for my Uncle

Barrie who's a teacher and lives in London, and I was trying to make up a funny poem to send as well. I had managed two really great lines but then I got stuck.

"There once was a vampire called Dracula,
Whose habits were really spectacular . . ."

I read it aloud to Angela and she rolled about on the rug laughing.

"It's brilliant, Charlie," she said. But she couldn't think of anything else, either.

"Here comes that drippy Julian," she said. "Ask him."

Julian came wandering aimlessly out of the back door, his head buried in a computer magazine. He looked paler than ever and had dark rings round his eyes as if he hadn't slept for a week. And although he's such a drip he's really quite bright, so I called him over and read him the poem.

He looked at me blankly and didn't even smile.

"Sorry," he said vaguely. "I'm not much good at that sort of thing. Anyway, I'm not feeling all that well. I was working until two o'clock this morning on my program." He gave a slight shiver in the cool morning air.

Angela looked at him, her head on one side.

"Sit down here and have a rest," she said kindly, and I looked at her in surprise. She grabbed Julian's wrist to pull him down beside her, but as soon as she touched him she gave a loud shriek and leapt into the air.

"Flippin' heck!" she breathed, rubbing her hand and staring at it as if it was burnt. "You're overloaded with static electricity. No wonder you don't feel well."

She gazed at him sympathetically. "Don't you know how dangerous it is?" she said. "You could blow yourself up."

Julian sat down forlornly, and put his head in his hands.

"I keep getting a shock off my dad's car," he said. "Is that something to do with it?"

"Of course it is," Angela assured him, and I wondered how she knew so much about it. "It happens to my Uncle Roger all the time. He works with computers and so he has to spend a lot of time on them. He has to drain off the build-up of static every weekend."

That drippy Julian sat gazing at Angela, and I could see he believed every word. Of course he didn't know Angela like I do. Nor did he know that she hasn't got an Uncle Roger who works with computers. She hasn't got an Uncle Roger at all.

"How do you mean, drain off the static?" he said, looking puzzled. "Is that possible?"

We had been doing a science project on electricity just before the end of term, and that's how Angela managed to sound so convincing.

"Water," she said. "All you need is a few buckets of water. It's one of the best conductors of electricity there is. You must know that yourself."

"You're right," said Julian, suddenly looking more cheerful. "What shall I do? Go for a swim?"

"That's no good," said Angela scornfully. "You need proper wires and things." She pushed Julian down onto the rug beside Daniel. "You wait there for a minute and don't go away. Charlie and me will fix everything."

She dragged me around the corner into Mrs Down's storeroom place where she keeps cleaning stuff and buckets and hoses and gardening tools.

"You can just stop looking so po-faced, Charlie

Ellis," she giggled. "We're not going to do him any harm. And it might even work."

She rummaged about until she found some lengths of copper wire and half a dozen plastic buckets. She shoved the buckets into my hands.

"Here, Charlie," she said. "Fill those at the tap and carry them round into the back garden. I'll get him wired up." And her blue eyes sparkled so much I hadn't the heart to refuse.

I filled two of the buckets and staggered round the back with them. Angela had Julian sitting meekly on a garden chair, and she was busy tying lengths of wire to his wrists and ankles.

"Oh, good. Thanks, Charlie," she said. "Just put them down here, will you."

My back was killing me by the time I'd carried all the other buckets of water. I never knew water was so heavy.

"What's it all for, anyway?" I asked.

Angela finished tying the last wire round Julian's head and began to arrange the buckets of water in a circle around him.

He didn't half look funny, I can tell you. He had wires tied to each wrist and ankle, one round his waist, and another round his forehead. The wires all had loose ends which dangled to the ground.

Angela carefully placed the free end of each wire into a bucket of water and stood back to admire the effect.

"That's it, I think," she said, satisfied. "That's how my Uncle Roger always does it. The static electricity runs out down these wires, and into the buckets of water. All right, Julian?"

"I feel a bit of a fool," muttered Julian glumly. "How long do I have to sit here like this?"

"Oh, not more than a couple of hours," said Angela airily. "You can read your magazine. But you must promise not to move until Charlie and me come back. Otherwise we'll have to start all over again. Come on, Charlie. We'll take Daniel for a little walk."

I put Daniel's lead on and the three of us went racing out into the street. Angela could hardly stand up for laughing, and I must admit I thought it was pretty funny myself. We were still giggling about it when our dads came back from their tennis, looking as pleased as anything with themselves.

"Come on, girls," they said. "Grab some warm sweaters and anoraks. We're all going fishing."

They had been down to the harbour and hired a small boat for the morning, and they were anxious not to waste any time. So we hurried indoors to fetch our waterproofs as the weather wasn't looking too promising, and it wasn't long before we were all chugging out across Shorelock Bay.

Daniel had never been in a boat before and was a bit nervous at first. But the sea was fairly calm and he settled down after a while and began to enjoy himself, barking now and again if a seagull flew too close and peering over the side of the boat to look at bits of seaweed floating by.

After a while we switched off the outboard engine and bobbed about in the middle of the bay, and we all had a great time. My dad is never happier than when he's fishing, and he whistled and sang and smoked his smelly old pipe to his heart's content. He didn't catch a single fish as usual, but Uncle Jim caught six fat mackerel, which he said he would ask Mrs Down to cook for our tea.

Angela lay back and trailed her fingers

dreamily in the water, watching the sailing boats and behaving herself for once. I tried just to relax and enjoy myself, but I kept on thinking about the poem I had been writing for my Uncle Barrie. It just wouldn't go out of my head.

"Dad, what rhymes with Dracula?" I asked, after racking my brains for a while. But he shook his head. He couldn't think of anything either.

Our lazy, happy morning was all at once brought to an end. A sudden flash of lightning and an ominous rumble of thunder made us all look at one another in alarm.

"Oo-er," said Angela, her face turning pale and her eyes going huge and round.

Great big drops of rain the size of golfballs began to fall, and we were glad my dad had made us bring our waterproofs. Uncle Jim quickly stowed away the fishing gear while my dad tried to get the engine started.

"Get a move on, Ted. We're all getting soaked," urged Uncle Jim, as my dad tugged time after time at the bit of string that was supposed to start the motor. But it only gave a sort of wheezing cough like my grandad in the mornings and then went silent.

"You have a go, if you can do any better," said my dad, looking flustered. "I think there's water in the carburettor." And I couldn't help giggling. He was a poet, after all.

I didn't giggle for long. The rain was coming down even harder and Angela, who's terrified of thunderstorms, shrieked loudly every time there was a lightning flash or a crash of thunder. Daniel barked at her every time she shrieked and it was absolute bedlam what with the thunder and the lightning and Angela screaming and the dog barking and my dad swearing and Uncle Jim shouting at him to get out of the way.

Our two dads stood up to change places and that's when the most awful thing of all happened. The boat gave a nasty lurch and Daniel, who had been jumping up and down in all the excitement, suddenly lost his balance and fell overboard with a splash. I gave a horrified wail and without thinking jumped straight in after him.

I heard them all shouting and then the cold water closed over my head. When I bobbed back to the surface again there was Daniel, his feet paddling frantically just a little way off. I grasped hold of his collar just as strong arms grabbed me and dragged me firmly back into the boat.

I lay on my back in the bottom of the boat, gasping and choking and spitting out salt water. Daniel shook himself hard and then began to lick my face. I sat up and hugged him thankfully, while three white faces stared down at me in relief.

"Thank God," said my dad quietly. "Charlie, don't ever do such a stupid thing again."

"Let's get this wretched engine started," said Uncle Jim. And this time it started first time.

Soon we were speeding towards the harbour. I sat in my wet things and shivered, and although they had piled extra clothing over me to keep me warm, my teeth were still chattering by the time we reached the shore. Angela gazed at me admiringly all the way back, and I could tell she thought it was ever such a brave thing to have done.

My dad made me run all the way from the boatyard to Harbour View. I had to get straight into a hot bath and then into bed, and I must say it was rather nice having everybody rushing around after me and making all that fuss and bringing me a special tasty lunch on a tray. My dad dried Daniel on one of Mrs Down's nice fluffy towels and then let him sit on my bed with me and beg scraps of my chicken.

Angela came to see if there was anything else I wanted before she went down for her own lunch. And it was only then that we remembered that drippy Julian.

"Oh, lord!" gasped Angela, clapping her hand over her mouth. "I wonder if he's still out there."

My bedroom window overlooked the back garden. I scrambled hastily out of bed and together we looked out. And you'll never believe it but that poor kid was still sitting there with his wires and his buckets, his magazine over his head to keep off the rain.

"What a twit," giggled Angela. "He must have sat there all through the thunderstorm. He must be really drippy by now." And she ran downstairs to release him.

And so I spent the rest of that day in bed, lazing about and reading and having another go at that rotten poem. I learnt later from my dad that Julian had been put to bed, too.

"He got caught out in the storm as well," said my dad, sitting on my bed and smoothing my hair off my face. "Doing some sort of daft experiment, I gather. Somebody's been having him on, if you ask me."

He looked at me suspiciously, but I just made my eyes go all wide and innocent the way Angela does, and he let it drop. He got up to go, and then turned at the door.

"By the way, Charlie," he said, "I've thought of a great rhyme for Dracula."

"What?" I said, grabbing paper and pencil hopefully. At last I could get this thing finished and give my poor brain a rest.

"Spectacular," said my dad, with a triumphant grin. And he looked so proud of himself I hadn't the heart to tell him.

"Thanks, Dad," I said, grinning back at him. "That's really good." And off he went, as pleased as Punch.

Chapter Eight

ALL too soon it was the last evening of our holiday. I had been to the hairdresser's in the afternoon and had my hair dyed back to its normal dark brown colour, so I was quite my old self again. My dad said I looked much better, but Angela made a face.

"You look dead ordinary and boring," she complained. "I liked it better the way it was."

"My mum wouldn't have done," I said. "She'd have had kittens."

We went downstairs together for our last evening meal at Harbour View, moaning to one another about how quickly the time had gone and wishing we had another week.

"We should really do something special tonight, as it's our last night," urged Angela. "Go on, Charlie. Why don't we dress up as ghosts and haunt that drippy Julian like we planned?"

"I think it's a horrible idea," I said. "Especially after he never told anyone it was us that tied him up with wires and things. He caught a stinking cold being left out there all that time in the rain."

Angela giggled heartlessly.

"Serves him right for being such a drip," she said. "Oh, go on, Charlie. Don't be so stuffy. It would be a great joke."

"No," I said firmly, and refused to listen to her any more. She sat next to me at the table and sulked all through the soup course, but I wouldn't give in. I had managed to stay out of trouble for a whole week, and I certainly didn't want to spoil it on the very last night.

The meal was tomato soup and crusty rolls,

followed by a lovely savoury shepherd's pie, so I ignored Angela and tucked into my food. Mrs Down came round with a big platter of vegetables.

"Now, girls," she cooed, waving her serving spoon. "What's it to be? Spinach or baked beans?"

Angela smiled up at her sweetly.

"I prefer baked beans, please, Mrs Down," she said. "But my friend Charlie likes spinach."

And before I could protest, Mrs Down had plonked a great nasty pile of horrible slimy green spinach on my plate.

"Good girl," she said. "That's what I like to see. Not many children will eat what's good for them these days. Mind you eat it all up now." She spooned a portion of baked beans over Angela's shepherd's pie and moved on.

I looked at my dad, but he was too busy persuading Mrs Down to give him both spinach and baked beans to take any notice of me.

"That was a lousy rotten trick," I hissed at Angela out of the side of my mouth. "You know I loathe spinach." And she blinked those huge blue eyes at me in surprise.

"Sorry, Charlie," she said innocently. "I must have been thinking of my cousin Sarah."

I scowled at her fiercely. I didn't believe a word of it, but there wasn't much I could do about it now. I stirred the horrible stuff into my shepherd's pie to disguise it as much as posible, and forced it down, mouthful by disgusting mouthful. It very nearly made me puke, but by the time my plate was empty I had planned my revenge. I was going to fix that Angela Mitchell, if it was the last thing I did.

After tea we did most of our packing so that we could get an early start the next morning. Then we all went for a last walk along the sea front.

It was a lovely evening. The air was clean and fresh and the light was all sort of golden. I stalked along, not speaking a word to Angela, and she looked more and more fed up the further we went. We walked a long way because our two dads wanted to make the most of their last chance to take photographs, and when we got back to Harbour View it was getting dark.

My dad yawned. "Think I'll have a bath and an early night," he said. "We've got a long drive tomorrow."

"Good idea," said Uncle Jim. "An early night won't do any of us any harm."

I couldn't wait to get upstairs and start putting my plan into action, and I was pleased my dad was going for a bath. He always likes to soak for at least half an hour, and it gave me a chance to have the bedroom to myself for a while.

"Goodnight, Angela," I smiled when we parted. And she squeezed my arm gratefully, glad that I'd forgiven her at last. Little did she know what horrors I was planning for her later on. It wasn't that drippy Julian who was going to get a visit from a ghost. It was her.

As soon as my dad went off to the bathroom, I got to work. I tore a page off my sketchpad, mixed some green watercolour paint, and painted a huge ghastly green grinning face. I had decided not to dress up as the white lady. What I had in mind was even more horrible than that.

When the paint was dry I cut out the oval face-shape with my nail scissors and stuck it over the strings of my dad's tennis racket with Sellotape. Then I got the small torch that my dad keeps by the bed in case of power cuts in the night and fastened it to the back of the strings behind the face. Then I switched on the torch and did a little dance of glee all by myself in the bedroom.

The torch shone through the paper and made the face light up with a ghastly green glow. It really was a terrifying sight, and it would look ten times worse coming at you suddenly in the dark. I couldn't wait to see Angela's face when she saw it. It would give her a taste of her own medicine for a change.

I had already made up my mind that I was sure to get into trouble. Angela would probably scream her head off and Uncle Jim was bound to wake up. But I had decided to take the risk. It would be worth the worst telling-off in the world to get my own back on Angela for once.

I heard my dad coming back along the landing so I switched off the torch and pushed the racket under my bed. Then I dived, still fully-dressed, under the covers.

I lay awake for a long time waiting for everybody in the house to go to sleep. I heard feet on the stairs, and people calling goodnight, and water flushing, and lights being switched out. I think I dozed for a while, because when I looked at the clock again it was just after midnight. My dad was snoring safely in the next bed. Now was the time.

I pulled the pale green bedspread off my bed and draped it over me with just enough of a gap near my eyes for me to peep out. Then I picked up the tennis racket, switched on the torch, and, keeping my hand hidden inside the folds of the bedspread, held the green glowing face in the air above my own.

I caught a glimpse of myself in the dressing-table mirror and had to stifle a shriek. I grinned foolishly in the dark. If it could frighten me, just think what it would do to Angela. I slowly turned the door handle and, hardly daring to breathe, I crept out onto the landing.

It was very creepy out there, I can tell you. The old house gave little creaks and groans as I made my way slowly along towards Angela's room, and I kept getting a horrible feeling that someone was behind me. Suppose there really was a ghost, I kept thinking. My heart did a somersault at the thought, and I almost gave up the whole idea and scarpered back to my safe little bed.

I took a few deep breaths to pull myself

together and crept on. Everything was lit up with a dim green glow in the light from my torch, and it made even the most innocent things look terrifying. Once I almost screamed when a large shape loomed up at me out of the darkness, but it was only somebody's golfbag, leaning against a wall.

I reached the end of the corridor at last, and turned the corner towards Angela's room. And then my mouth went dry and my hair stood on end and my feet glued themselves to the carpet because something was coming towards me from the opposite direction.

I opened my mouth to scream but not a sound came out and I've never been so scared in my life. I was looking at the very thing I'd been dreading all along. The ghost of the white lady.

The figure drifted towards me along the landing, in a long white gown that reached the ground. A white veil covered its face and head, and as it drew nearer I saw its deathly pale hands knotting and unknotting in a kind of frenzied anguish. But the worst thing of all was the noise it was making.

"Oh, woe, woe, woe," it moaned, over and

over again, in a thin, high-pitched wail that made my teeth start to chatter. "Oh, woe, woe, woe."

And then all of a sudden it saw me standing there in the middle of the corridor. It stopped wailing and stared at me for one ghastly moment with its mouth opened wide like a fish gasping for air. And then it screamed, a long unearthly scream that echoed round the old house and made my blood run cold.

And that's when I suddenly got my voice back and started to scream, too. And there we were shrieking our heads off at the tops of our voices as if we were being murdered and doors started opening and lights went on and people started hurrying out onto the landing in their pyjamas and Uncle Jim arrived and then my dad and they grabbed us and shook us and shouted at us to calm down and that's when we both came to our senses.

I didn't half feel stupid, I can tell you. The white lady wasn't a ghost at all. It was Angela, in her dad's white towelling dressing-gown and her white chiffon scarf, her hands whitened with talcum powder.

"Charlie!" she gasped, when my dad pulled

the bedspread off me and ripped the painted green face off the tennis racket. "You didn't half give me a fright. I was coming to play a trick on you."

We gazed at one another sheepishly, while everybody muttered and argued and complained about their sleep being disturbed by unruly kids and they were all making so much noise that at first they didn't hear Mrs Down standing there shouting for silence and she had to bang on the floor with my dad's tennis racket and he swears it's never been the same since.

"What on earth is going on here?" she demanded, her voice coming out all squeaky with rage. We all turned to stare at her, and she must have rushed out of her room in a hurry because she had forgotten to put in her false teeth and I've never seen anything so funny in my life.

And of course it was my dad who laughed first. He's never very good at keeping a straight face at moments like that. He laughed like anything at my cousin Oliver's christening when the vicar accidentally dropped the baby in the font. And once my dad starts hooting and honking it doesn't take long before everybody else joins in.

Soon all the Harbour View guests were having a good old chuckle, and even the two frowsy schoolteachers managed a titter.

Mrs Down was livid. Her mouth went so thin it almost disappeared altogether. She stood there with her arms folded, glowering like a toothless grizzly, while my dad explained that it had all been just a childish prank. And she had the cheek to order us out of her house by ten o'clock the next morning.

"The silly woman must have forgotten we're leaving anyway," grinned my dad, as we all trooped back to bed. And the amazing thing is, both dads were so amused at the whole thing that we got off completely scot-free. My dad just couldn't stop laughing about it. He was still sniggering when he finally switched out the light and climbed into bed.

"You're a proper scallywag, our Charlie, and that's a fact," he chuckled affectionately, and I smiled to myself in the dark.

Angela got up before me the next morning, and she was coming in the front door just as I was on my way out to take Daniel for his walk. She put her arm through mine, as friendly as pie.

"Come on, Charlie, I'll come with you," she said. "Wasn't it great last night? That green face you made was brilliant. I thought I was going to die."

"What have you been up to, out so early?" I demanded. But as usual she wouldn't tell me anything. We gave Daniel his walk, ate a hasty breakfast under the cold beady eye of Mrs Down, and loaded all our stuff into the car as fast as we could.

And as we backed out of the Harbour View car park, I noticed a very strange thing. Mrs Down's tiny front garden was full of people. They had rugs and picnic hampers and dogs and balls and children and transistor radios blaring pop music.

"Look, Dad," I said. "What's going on? Is Mrs Down having a fête?"

"It would be a fate worse than death if she did," snorted my dad, and Angela giggled in the back seat.

We slowed down to get a better look as we went past, just as another crowd of people arrived and went through the gate. And that's when we realised what was happening.

On the front of the gate, hiding Mrs Down's

"Private" sign, was a notice. And printed on the notice, in Angela's unmistakeable untidy scrawl were these words:

GARDEN OPEN TO THE PUBLIC.
PICK-KNICKERS WELCOME
ADMISHUN FREE.

We all burst out laughing and Angela went pink. And as we drove away along the street we saw Mrs Down rushing out of the front door, shouting and stamping and tearing her hair.

"Serves her right, the silly old bat," said Angela with satisfaction, and I knew that was one place where we wouldn't be welcome ever again.

Not that I cared. I sat back in my seat with my arm round Daniel and I felt suddenly quite fond of Angela for a change. We'd really had a lot of fun this holiday and she'd managed to keep her promise after all. She hadn't got me into trouble, not even once.

It only goes to show that she can do it when she wants to. But somehow I can't help wondering what I'm going to be in for when we get back to school. She hasn't made any promises about that. Oh well. Roll on September.

Paddington

Michael Bond

A very rare sort of bear once stowed away on a journey from Peru, and just turned up on Paddington station wearing a label which read: "Please look after this bear. Thank you." So Paddington came to live with Mrs and Mrs Brown, and became London's most famous marmalade-eating, duffel-coated bear!

Lions

The Demon Bike Rider   Robert Leeson   £2.25
There was a ghost on Barker's Bonk: a horned demon that made a terrible howling noise as it glided along in the dusk – on a bicycle. Mike and friends thought the bike-riding ghost could only be a joke until they saw and heard it; then suddenly they were running so fast there was no time to laugh.

Challenge in the Dark   Robert Leeson   £2.50
His first week at the new school is a challenge for Mike Baxter – not least when he makes an enemy of Steven Taylor and his bullying older brother, Spotty Sam. But the dare that both accept, of staying in the cold, dark silence of a disused underground shelter, leads to an unexpected friendship.

Wheel of Danger   Robert Leeson   £2.25
When Mike and his friends discover a disused mill out on the moors, it offers an exciting challenge: to get the water wheel working again. But the summer holiday adventure turns to danger when the mill race floods – and three of the children are trapped in the wheel house, with the water rising fast . . .

Lions

Josie Smith   Magdalen Nabb   £2.75
Josie Smith lives with her mum in an industrial town; she
is a resourceful, independent little girl who always does
what she thinks best, but often lands herself in trouble.

Josie Smith at the Seaside   Magdalen Nabb   £2.75
Josie Smith makes friends with a girl called Rosie
Margaret; with the donkey, Susie; and with a big friendly
dog called Jimmie, who swims off with Josie Smith's new
bucket.

Josie Smith at School   Magdalen Nabb   £2.75
More muddles and misunderstandings for Josie Smith.
She is horribly late for lessons when she tries to get a
present for her new teacher. And then she helps her new
friend to write a story and completely forgets to do her
own homework!

Josie Smith and Eileen   Magdalen Nabb   £2.75
Josie Smith doesn't always like Eileen because Eileen has
things that Josie Smith longs for – a birthday party, a bride
doll, and the chance to be a bridesmaid in a long shiny
pink frock. But Josie is happy in the end.

You can see Josie Smith in the Granada TV serial, *Josie
Smith*.

Lions

Hoppity Gap by Chris Powling
£2.99

Ellie is tired of being dragged from town to town
by her famous, showbiz father. One day, feeling
lonely, she follows a strange dog through the city
to a bleak wasteland where she meets a
mysterious gang.

ELF 61 by Chris Powling
£2.99

Tina's gran and her beloved car, ELF 61, are staying
with Tina's family. Tina watches and watches the
car, and the more she does so, the more she is
convinced there's something strange about it.
Tina's gran knows there is, and she persuades Tina
to accompany her on a hair-raising and magical
journey in ELF 61.

Fancy Nancy by Ruth Craft
£2.50

Have you ever wondered how to cope with a
difficult guest, or how to amuse yourself at a
boring party? Fancy Nancy has the answers in
these lively and imaginative stories of her life at
school, at play and at home with her family.

Fancy Nancy In Disguise by Ruth Craft
£2.50

Fancy Nancy, that very real little girl who has the
knack of spotting the unusual, is back again. This
time she's in search of a new disguise, because she
knows everyone will recognise her old one.

Carrot Top   Nigel Gray   £2.99
Carrot Top! That's what all the kids call Melinda, a little girl with a bright personality and bright red hair to match. And whether it's helping Dad with wallpapering, playing with her friends or celebrating her birthday, every day is a new adventure.

Operation Pedal Paw   Trevor Harvey   £2.50
Andrew and his friend Warren are determined to find Andrew's stolen bike – and five rabbits which have also mysteriously disappeared. But Andrew steals back the wrong rabbits, with disastrous consequences!

Speedy Fred   Josephine Haworth   £2.99
Fred doesn't like staying with his grandfather in the country, and he's terrified of Uncle Joe's horse, Black Bob. And when Grandad's bike runs out of petrol and they're stuck on the moor, guess who has to ride and get help?

Dangleboots   Dennis Hamley   £2.99
Dangleboots – that's what everyone on the football team calls Andy Matthews, because he's so useless. Until the day he buys the little dangling football boots off a market stall, and suddenly things start to go right. It's great at first, but then peculiar and rather frightening things begin to happen . . .

Lions

All these books are available at your local bookshop or newsagent, or can be ordered from the publishers.

To order direct from the publishers just tick the titles you want and fill in the form below:

Name _____

Address _____

_____

Send to: Collins Children's Cash Sales
          PO Box 11
          Falmouth
          Cornwall
          TR10 9EN

Please enclose a cheque or postal order or debit my Visa/Access –

Credit card no:

Expiry date:

Signature:

– to the value of the cover price plus:

UK: 80p for the first book, and 20p per copy for each additional book ordered to a maximum charge of £2.00.

BFPO: 80p for the first book, and 20p per copy for each additional book.

Overseas and Eire: £1.50 for the first book, £1.00 for the second book, thereafter 30p per book.

Young Lions reserve the right to show new retail prices on covers which may differ from those previously advertised in the text or elsewhere.

Young Lions